For Aunt Sue—the best sister I know.

Sindy McKay

Parent's Introduction

We Both Read is the first series of books designed to invite parents and children to share the reading of a story by taking turns reading aloud. This "shared reading" innovation, which was developed in conjunction with early reading specialists, invites parents to read the more sophisticated text on the left-hand pages, while children are encouraged to read the right-hand pages, which have been written at one of three early reading levels.

Reading aloud is one of the most important activities parents can share with their child to assist their reading development. However, *We Both Read* goes beyond reading *to* a child and allows parents to share reading *with* a child. *We Both Read* is so powerful and effective because it combines two key elements in learning: "showing" (the parent reads) and "doing" (the child reads). The result is not only faster reading development for the child, but a much more enjoyable and enriching experience for both!

Most of the words used in the child's text should be familiar to them. Others can easily be sounded out. You may find it helpful to read the entire book aloud yourself the first time, then invite your child to participate on the second reading. Also note that the parent's text is preceded by a "talking parent" icon: ☺ ; and the child's text is preceded by a "talking child" icon: ☺ .

We Both Read books is a fun, easy way to encourage and help your child to read—and a wonderful way to start your child off on a lifetime of reading enjoyment!

We Both Read: The Big Tan Van

———————————————

Text Copyright © 2001 by Sindy McKay
Illustrations Copyright © 2001 by Meredith Johnson
All rights reserved

We Both Read® is a trademark of Treasure Bay, Inc.

Published by Treasure Bay, Inc.
40 Sir Francis Drake Blvd.
San Anselmo, CA 94960 USA

PRINTED IN SINGAPORE

Library of Congress Catalog Card Number: 2001 131569

Hardcover ISBN: 1-891327-35-6
Paperback ISBN: 1-891327-36-4

05 06 07 08 09 / 10 9 8 7 6 5 4 3 2

We Both Read® Books
Patent No. 5,957,693

Visit us online at:
www.webothread.com

WE BOTH READ®

The
Big Tan Van

By Sindy McKay

Illustrated by Meredith Johnson

TREASURE BAY

Aunt Susie is my auntie.
She's someone you should meet.
Mom says she's unusual,
But I just think she's neat!

Aunt Susie's an explorer.
She travels when she can.
To get to where she's going
She drives a big . . .

... tan van.

My mom is Aunt Sue's sister—
The only one she's got.
My mother is so quiet.
Aunt Susie is so <u>not</u>!

Sue wears **big** boots of rubber,
A large hat and a vest.
Atop her hat is sitting

A **big** hen in a nest.

Now you may think that's zany—
A big hen in a hat.
But my Aunt Sue *is* zany.
I think her van proves that!

Way up upon the rooftop
There sits a great big dish.
And when I look inside it—

I see a pig and fish!

The headlights are amazing—
They're colorful and bright.
The fuzzy bright green fenders
Are really quite a sight!

The handles all wear mittens.
The tires all wear socks.
The engine is made up of

A lot of red hot rocks!

Sue slides the van door open
And tells me, "Step inside!"
And then I know I'm in for
A really awesome ride!

Aunt Susie **makes** me comfy.
The tan van is such fun!
The best-est part of all is—

The sun will **make** it run!

We **find** a place to visit—
Aunt Susie's favorite store.
This store is like no other
That I've been to before!

Aunt Sue tries on a long scarf,
An apron, and a fan.
She looks inside the pockets

To **find** a cat and pan!

I try some silly pants on,
Then pull on snakeskin boots.
I think that I look funny—
Aunt Sue says I look cute!

"Just be prepared," says Susie.
She knows just what to get.
She buys us both a pair of stilts,

So we will not get wet.

The store has sports equipment
Like I have never seen!
For experts and beginners
And all of us between.

Aunt Susie just loves baseball.
She finds the perfect mitt.
She bowls a ball right to me.

I give the ball a hit.

"It's time for us to move on,"
Aunt Sue says with a smile.
So to the van we hurry
And travel for awhile.

The park is where we're going
So we can take a **jog**.
We take along her Froggy.

We **jog** on a big log!

Then Sue pulls out a basket.
She says, "Let's take a break!"
We have a pleasant picnic
Way far out on the lake.

Now this may sound quite silly
And not make sense to some,
But Susie likes to chew on

A big bun full of gum!

Her Froggy likes mosquitoes.
He covers them with cheese.
But I prefer the hot dogs—
The kind that don't have fleas!

And when we're finished eating,
Aunt Susie has a whim.
Since **all** our food is eaten,

We **all** can take a swim!

And when we're finished swimming,
We climb back in the van.
We set out for adventure
To seek more fun again!

We travel down an alley,
And I hear bagpipes **play**.
Aunt Sue says, "Sounds like Gertie,

And she can **play** all day!"

We stop in for a visit.
A great big crowd is there.
I like the way they're dancing
Like no one has a care!

Aunt Sue sings very loudly
And shares a dance with me.
But when she yells out "Maple!"

We all must be a tree!

Then Sue gets an idea
The kind you just can't stop.
Aunt Susie feels inspired!
She wants us all to hop!

And so we all start hopping.
We hop and hop with pride.
We go on hopping up and down

And then hop side to side!

It's time for us to go now.
I ask Aunt Sue, "Where to?"
The answer to my question—
"It's time to see the zoo!"

So down the **road** we travel—
Aunt Sue, me, and a toad.
Until we hit a problem—

A big hole in the **road**!

But nothing stops Aunt Susie—
We press on to the zoo!
And when at last we get **there**,
The greeters shout, "Yoo hoo!"

The greeters wear pink outfits.
They smile, as a rule.
They send us to the counter,

And **there** we find a mule!

I see so many creatures—
A tiger and a skunk.
An elephant's unpacking
His suitcase and his trunk.

That horse is in pajamas.
That lion wears a wreath!

That bat has got a cape on—
And has ten sets of teeth!

The ducks are wearing raincoats.
The monkeys are in suits.
The rhino horns play music,
So you hear lots of "toots."

Aunt Susie says the **brown bear**
Is really a great dude.

But when we broke his bike up
The big **brown bear** was rude.

The zoo has much to offer,
And I could **look** all day!
But Susie is impatient—
"We must be on our way!"

We've been so many places.
So many we have not.

And so we get the map out
And **look** for a new spot!

Deciding where to travel
Is really very hard.
Why, we could go to Egypt,
Or maybe Scotland Yard.

Or we could go to Venus—
Aunt Susie says we can.
Anywhere is possible

VENUS

SIERRAS

CHICAGO

NE
YO

In my Aunt Sue's tan van!

If you liked
***The Big Tan Van*, here are two other**
***We Both Read*® Books you are sure to enjoy!**

Kibu is a young member of the Masai tribe in Africa. When Kibu is told he is too small to go on the lion hunt, he decides to prove that he too can be a mighty lion hunter. He sets off into the wilderness to find the biggest lion of all, Father Lion. With the help of some animal friends he meets along the way, Kibu hopes to outsmart and capture Father Lion.

To see all the We Both Read books that are available,
just go online to **www.webothread.com**

A very whimsical tale of a boy and his dog and
their fantastic dreamland adventures. This delightful
tale features fun and easy to read text for the very
beginning reader, such as "pigs that dig", "fish on a
dish", and a "dog on a frog." Both children and their
parents will love this newest addition to the We Both
Read series!